A LITTLE OWL BOOK

THE PIED PIPER

by Clive Hopwood

illustrated by Alan Linsdell

WORLD

Once upon a time there was a town called Hamelin. It was a happy place where children laughed and played, and their mummies and daddies worked hard and were both healthy and content.

Then one day the rats came. They were wicked creatures, all black or brown, with long tails and sharp teeth. They ate the people's food, made nests in their houses, and scared away all the cats. The people were afraid.

The people went to the Mayor, whose job it was to look after the town, and told him the rats were eating them out of house and home. They asked him to make all the rats go away.

The Mayor just didn't know what to do, and nor did any of his counsellors. "If we do not get rid of these rats," he said, "they will destroy the town." But nobody could think of a good idea.

Just then, the door opened and a strange man, dressed all in red and yellow, came in. In his hand he carried a whistle pipe. "I have come to help rid you of the rats," he said.

"My name is the Pied Piper," said the man, "and I can charm all creatures living beneath the sun with the magic music I play on my pipe."

"If you will promise to pay me one thousand guilders," he continued, "I will charm all your rats away, and make Hamelin a happy place once more." The Mayor and his counsellors were overjoyed.

They were so pleased, they would not hear of him accepting so small a reward. "Why," exclaimed the Mayor, "if you will make the rats leave Hamelin, we will pay you not one, but *fifty* thousand guilders!"

The bargain struck, the Pied Piper went out into the street and began to play a strange, haunting tune upon his pipe. No sooner had he started than rats came scurrying from every nook and cranny in the town.

Down the street he led them, the rats all following without a thought, so enchanted were they with his music. Over hill and dale they went, until at length they came to a river, whose waters ran swift and deep.

The music seemed to speak to them of all manner of food if they did but follow the Pied Piper. Too late they realised it was all a dream, and every last one was drowned beneath the swirling waters.

The people of Hamelin danced for joy they were so happy to be free of the rats, and long into the night the celebrations lasted, with feasting and singing and merry-making. Even the Mayor and his counsellors were happy.

His task complete, the Pied Piper returned and went at once to claim his reward. But now that all the rats were gone, the Mayor did not care about the Pied Piper, and would not pay him.

The Pied Piper became angry. "Ungrateful people! I have rid your town of rats, and yet you will not keep your promise to pay me!" He turned to go. "You will see it is not the only tune I play."

This said, he went out once more into the street and began to play upon his pipe. Now, from every house in the town, the children came running to hear the weird and wonderful melody he played.

Their parents could do nothing but watch helplessly as the Pied Piper led away their children, all dancing merrily to his tune. Loudly the parents cried, thinking their children would be drowned just like the rats.

But when he reached the river, the Pied Piper took them along a path which led to a mountainside. "Surely he will let them go now," thought the parents, "for they can go no further."

To their surprise the mountainside opened up. The music promised the children a wonderful land where everything was new and strange and happiness reigned all the year round. So in they went after the Pied Piper.

After all the children had gone inside, the mountain closed up behind them. They were all gone. All, that is, except one little boy who had a lame foot, and could not keep up with the others.

When he saw that he had been left behind, he sat down and cried, for he had so longed to join his friends in that magic land. Now he was alone, for not one single boy or girl remained in Hamelin.

And the people of Hamelin were sad too. No longer was the sound of laughing children heard in the streets, and although they were no longer plagued with rats, they found no joy in life without the children they loved.

The Mayor sent messengers all over the land to seek the Pied Piper, promising him anything he wanted if he would only bring back the children . . . but no trace of him could be found.

Nothing was ever seen of the children again, though it was said that some still heard the sound of their laughter, and the Pied Piper's haunting tune, whenever they walked by that mountainside.

And that same lame boy grew up, a sadder but wiser man, vowing that, all his life, if he should ever make a promise he would always keep his word.